Carol Jean Sc

Merry Animal Tales

Merry Animal Tales

by Madge A. Bigham

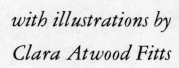

with illustrations by
Clara Atwood Fitts

LITTLE, BROWN AND COMPANY
Boston · Toronto

Contents

chapter one

Blackie's Fright

IN a garret of a great big house on Madison Square lived Mr. and Mrs. Blackrat and their little son Blackie. They thought Blackie was the finest fellow in all the world. He had a soft glossy coat, and a long slender tail, and a pair of the merriest black eyes that you ever saw.

Of course there were other rats living in the garret on Madison Square—more than a hundred, I guess—mothers and fathers, grandmothers and grandfathers, aunts and uncles and cousins, besides great-great-great-grandfathers and great-great-great-grandmothers.

They all lived in the garret together; and fine times they had, too. They scampered over the garret floor. They tipped down the winding stairway that led down, down, down to the big cool pantry. There the fat cook kept all the cake and pies and cheese and butter and other nice things which rats like to eat.

It was in the pantry that they had the greatest fun. But something sorrowful happened one day, for a great big gray cat came to live in the house on Madison Square. That was dreadful news to all the rats, I can tell you.

"Oh, dear, dear," they
said, "why couldn't that
gray cat go somewhere else
to live? Now he will always
be after us!"

So, while the cat liked
the rats, the rats did not
like the cat. Every time
they saw the tip of his nose
or even the end of his tail,
away they would run, hel-
ter-skelter, pell-mell, head
over heels, one right after

the other, trying to get out of the way of the great big gray cat. It would frighten them almost to death!

But I started out to tell you about Blackie—Mr. and Mrs. Blackrat's little son. He had never seen a cat in all his life, and his mother had told him she hoped he never would. But of course he did, and it happened this way:

One morning Blackie was out in the back yard playing under the lumber pile, and all at once his mother heard him yell, and his father heard him squeal, and then Blackie came scampering up the back steps into the garret. A tiny piece of his tail had been bitten off!

"Dear me, how dreadful!" said Mrs.

Blackrat. "A piece of your beautiful tail!
What have you been doing, Blackie?
Come right here and tell me all about
it!"

Blackie wiped away his tears and said, "Well, Mother, I was just playing 'hopping' under the lumber pile, when all at once I saw two queer things looking at me that I had never seen before. One of them was ugly and the other was pretty."

"Tell me how the pretty one looked," said Mrs. Blackrat.

"Beautiful," said Blackie, "almost like us, Mother, only ever so much larger. It came creeping, creeping towards me. It had a soft gray coat, and a pretty waving tail, and pink ears, and soft paws, and the brightest, kindest eyes. I was sure whatever it was it would be the very best friend to rats. I was just waiting to speak to it, when the other ugly thing frightened me so I ran away."

"Tell me how the ugly thing looked," said Mrs. Blackrat.

"Oh, he looked dreadful!" said Blackie, with a shudder. "He had the ugliest head, with a bill that pecked. He had just two feet, with the sharpest claws. He was all covered over with spotted feathers, and he had ugly wings, that went 'flap, flap,' at his sides. When he saw me, he stretched out his great long neck and said, 'Cock-a doodle-do! Cock-a-doodle-do! Kut, kut, kut, kut, kut, kut, kut, kut!' He made such a noise that it frightened me out of my senses. I came running up the steps to you, and as I ran something bit my tail.

I know it must have been that ugly, crowing thing!"

"Oh, Blackie, Blackie!" said Mrs. Blackrat. "What a wonder that you ever came back to me alive! You poor little thing, you do not know a cat from a rooster! Don't you know the thing you saw and called ugly was your best friend, and really saved your life when he frightened you away by crowing? He was only a good old rooster, and would not even hurt a flea.

"But the other thing you saw, Blackie, and thought so beautiful—that was the horrid gray cat you have heard me tell about. Cats are never friends to rats. Cats eat every rat they lay their claws on. It's

10

a wonder the gray cat did not eat you just now, instead of the tip end of your tail. Blackie, Blackie, suppose you had never come back to me! You see," said Mrs. Blackrat, "we cannot always tell our friends by their *looks*.Come here, my son, and let me tie up the end of your beautiful tail."

Then Blackie nestled close to his mother's side, and promised never to play under the lumber pile again, although he would have liked to thank Mr. Rooster for saving his life.

chapter two

The Rat Meeting

A FEW DAYS after Blackie's tail was bitten Mr. Blackrat came through the door of his home as fast as lightning.

"Why, what can be the matter, my dear? Why so much hurry?" said Mrs. Blackrat, looking up from her work.

"Matter?" said Mr. Blackrat. "I almost lost my head just now—why, my life is growing to be a daily misery to me. I cannot even go into the pantry for a slice of cake, or a sip of cream, or a bit of cheese, without being jumped at by

that old gray cat. If we rats ever expect
to have any more peace, we have just got
to get rid of that cat, or move out!"

"Yes," said Mrs. Blackrat, "I know it.

Life is difficult with that hateful cat here. Why, Blackie has been afraid to go out to play since his tail was bitten. I wish we could do something to get rid of that cat."

"And we shall!" said Mr. Blackrat, snapping his sharp black eyes. "I'll not run from that cat another time! Blackie, my son go around to every hole in the garret and tell every rat you see to meet me tonight at twelve o'clock on the top pantry shelf. We will talk over a plan to get rid of that gray cat. Run, my son, run!

So Blackie ran, and stopped at every door, and told every rat what Mr. Blackrat had said. Sure enough, that night at twelve o'clock all the rats in the Madison Square mansion came to the pantry dressed in their Sunday best.

They sat in rows on the top pantry shelf, and talked and talked and talked about how they could get rid of the old gray cat.

At last Mr. Blackrat said, as he stroked his long gray whiskers, "Ladies and gentlemen, a fine idea has struck me, and I have the best of plans. Why not hang a bell around the gray cat's neck? Wherever she goes the bell will ring. We can then hear her coming, and get out of the way in a graceful manner, without falling over one another and almost breaking our necks in the scuffle!"

"Good! Good! How wonderful! How wise!" cried all the rats. "A most excellent plan indeed!"

"I think so," said Mr. Blackrat. "Now all who are in favor of this plan will please stand on their heads! And *every* rat stood on his head, with tail on high— even little Blackie and his friends Snowwhite and Brownie and Ringtail.

"Good!" said Mr. Blackrat, when they had all turned back. "Now, one more question: All who are willing to hang that bell around the gray cat's neck will please stand on their heads." Not a single rat moved—not even Blackie, nor Snowwhite, nor Brownie, nor Ringtail. They all sat still and blinked and looked at one another.

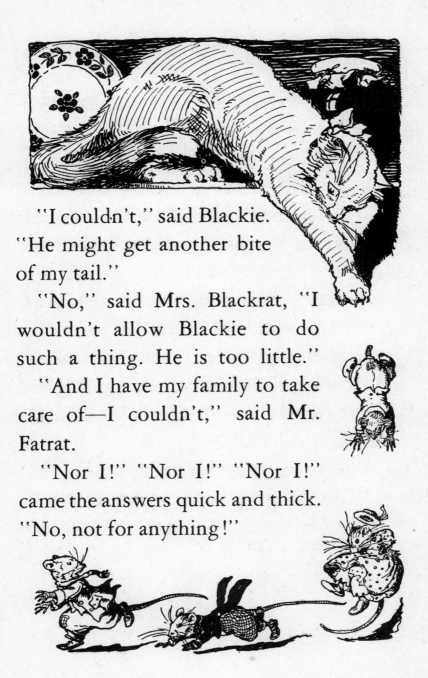

"I couldn't," said Blackie. "He might get another bite of my tail."

"No," said Mrs. Blackrat, "I wouldn't allow Blackie to do such a thing. He is too little."

"And I have my family to take care of—I couldn't," said Mr. Fatrat.

"Nor I!" "Nor I!" "Nor I!" came the answers quick and thick. "No, not for anything!"

"Why be afraid?" said Mr. Blackrat. "We are not cowards!"

Just then something came creeping, creeping through the pantry door, and with one great bounce the big gray cat sprang to the pantry shelf. How those rats did scatter! With Mr. Blackrat in the lead, they tumbled helter-skelter, pell-mell, head over heels one right after the other in the most disgraceful manner!

The big gray cat laughed and laughed as he curled down in Mr. Blackrat's seat on the pantry shelf.

"Why be afraid, my friends?" he said. "Hang a bell on my neck, indeed! Ha, ha!"

chapter three

Blackie's Country Home

ONE NIGHT after Blackie had gone to bed Mr. and Mrs. Blackrat sat talking by their fire.

"You see, my dear," said Mr. Blackrat, "none of us will ever be able to hang a bell around that gray cat's neck. The only thing we can do now is to move away to the country. I know where there is a most beautiful log house for rent, and the sooner we move the better."

"Very well," said Mrs. Blackrat, with a sigh. "You know I always liked city

19

life, though,
and it is hard that I
have to give it up just
for a horrid old cat. But then, the sum-
mertime is coming, and maybe the country air will be good for Blackie's sore

tail. If you really wish to go we will tell our friends good-by and leave tomorrow."

"All right," said Mr. Blackrat, rubbing his paws together, "that is better. You are a dear little wife to move to the country just to please Blackie and me." Then they both tumbled into bed and were soon fast asleep.

Sure enough, they moved the very next day. Blackie loved the country. His new home was a great hollow log. It was hollow all the way from the front door to the back door. Outside pretty vines climbed up and almost covered the log house.

Best of all, no big gray cat was there to bite Blackie's tail and scare him. He

just played and played all the time—
except when he studied his lessons—
"leap frog" and "hopping" and "jump-
ing" and "hiding" and everything else,
from one end of that log to the other.

One morning, while Mr. and Mrs.
Blackrat were planting peas, Blackie
thought he would take a walk in the
woods. So off he went, skipping down
a little winding path as happy as could be.

By and by he came to something ly-
ing on the grass—something very large
and soft and gray. It wasn't the gray cat.
It was ever so much larger than a cat—it
was a big lion, fast asleep on the grass.
But Blackie had never seen a lion and he
did not know what it was.

He thought it was just a little hill.

"Ho! Ho! What a nice little soft hill,"
Blackie said, "I believe I will stop here
and play 'sliding down.'" He crawled
up on Mr. Lion's back and was having
the finest time sliding. But all at once
Mr. Lion woke up just as Blackie was
starting down again.

"Goodness gracious me!" said Mr.
Lion, scratching, "that feels like a very
big flea running around on my back; let
me see." He reached up his big fat paw

and grabbed Blackie by the ears. Then he pulled him down and held him tight. When he saw it was only a little rat, he was so surprised he didn't know what to do.

Blackie was surprised too, and afraid, but he said, "Oh, do excuse me and let me go. I never will slide down your back any more. I thought you were just a hill!"

"A hill!" said Mr. Lion. "Ha, ha, ha!" and he opened his mouth so wide and laughed so loud it frightened Blackie more than ever. "Oh," Blackie said, "I know my mother wants to see me right now—please let me go!"

"You poor little rat," said Mr. Lion, "I guess she does, and I'm sorry I frightened you. Run on home to your mother, and be careful next time what kind of hills you slide down!"

"Thank you ever so much for letting me go," said Blackie. "Some day I will do something kind for you."

"Pshaw!" said Mr. Lion, and he laughed again. "You are too little to do anything for a big lion. Now run on home, and let me finish my nap."

So away scampered Blackie down the forest path, just as fast as he could go. When he got home he told his mother the most wonderful tale about sliding down a hill and seeing the grandfather of all the cats. Mrs. Blackrat did not believe one word of it. She just said, "Oh, Blackie, hush! You have *such* an imagination!

chapter four

Mr. Lion

ONE MORNING it rained and rained at Blackie's house, and Blackie couldn't go out to play. His mother had a headache, and everything he did, his mother said "Don't!" If he ran to the front door she said "Don't!" If he ran to the back door she said "Don't!" If he climbed up the side of the wall she said "Don't!" If he climbed down the side of the wall she said "Don't!" If he played "leapfrog" or "hiding" or "marbles," she said "Don't!" Blackie did not

26

know what to do! He was having a dreadful time.

Well, at last Blackie ran out of the back door and underneath the house to play. He made a pretty playhouse, all by himself, and just as he finished the sun came out.

"Oh, now," said Blackie, "I believe I will run out in the woods to find some pretty moss for a carpet and sticks to make a table. It has stopped raining and Mother won't care!"

While Blackie was hunting moss and sticks, he heard a great noise farther off in the woods, "Ro-ar! Come and help me! Ro-ar-r-r—Help me!"

Blackie listened and listened. "What

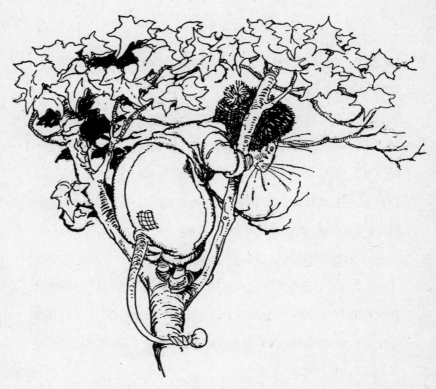

can it be?" he said. "It seems to me I've heard that voice before. Where was it?"

Then he climbed a high tree and looked and looked, and what do you think he saw?

It was Mr. Lion. He was tied down to the ground in a strong net of ropes, so tight he couldn't even stand up. He lay kicking on the ground, roaring like thunder.

At first Blackie felt afraid and wanted to run home. Then he remembered how kind Mr. Lion had been to him when he caught him sliding down his back. Blackie slipped down the tree and ran as quickly as he could to Mr. Lion's side. "What is it?" said Blackie. "Are you in trouble? Can I help you?"

"Help me!" roared Mr. Lion. "How can a little mite like you help anything? Don't you see how I am tied down here with these thousand ropes—so tight I cannot move? You know you can't help me!" And then Mr. Lion opened his big mouth and roared some more.

"Oh," said Blackie, "please don't do that! I can help you, just wait a minute. I will show you what my sharp teeth can do. I can cut those ropes in a little while."

"You can?" said Mr. Lion. "Well, I can't believe it! Aren't you the little rat I caught in the woods not long ago?"

"Yes," said Blackie, "I'm the very one, and I've come to help you now. Watch and see what I can do!" So Blackie went to work with his sharp little teeth, and gnawed and gnawed until his jaws ached.

"Almost through?" said Mr. Lion.

"I shall be so glad to be free once more."

"Almost through," said Blackie, "only one more rope. Now! See if you can stand up." And sure enough, Mr. Lion gave a big shake, and stretched,

and stood up straight. He stretched and stretched, and oh, it felt so good he just laughed a great roaring laugh.

"Oh-o-o! What a great big mouth you have!" said Blackie. "Do you bite?"

"Oh, no," said Mr. Lion, "not little fellows like you. Indeed, I thank you very much for helping me out of my trouble. I never dreamed a little mite like you could help a great big lion!"

"Oh, that was easy to do," said Blackie. "I said I was going to help you some day. Now I must run home; my mother will wonder where I am"

"That's so," said Mr. Lion, "and I must be going too, for Mrs. Lion will be wondering where I am."

So Mr. Lion ran through the woods to tell Mrs. Lion all about it, and little Blackie skipped through the woods to tell his mother all about it. But do you know, his mother wouldn't believe anything he said about it this time, either! She wouldn't! She just said, "Oh, pshaw, Blackie, don't! Your imagination will kill me yet!"

Then Blackie went off and sat on the back steps, and wondered and wondered what imagination meant.

chapter five

Mrs. Blackrat's House Party

MRS. BLACKRAT'S country house looked so pretty, with the vines climbing all about it, that she kept wishing her city friends might see it. She was talking about it one morning at the breakfast table, and Mr. Blackrat said, "My dear, why not give a house party?"

"That will be the very thing!" said Mrs. Blackrat. "We will invite all our friends from the big house on Madison Square. I know they will enjoy a week of fresh air and sunshine, and peace

from that horrid cat. We will invite them
this very day!"

"Do, Mother," said Blackie, "and ask
Ringtail and Brownie and Snowwhite
too!"

Mrs. Blackrat held up a warning finger. "How often have I told you not to speak unless you are spoken to? Of course they will be invited. Now, you eat your breakfast and keep quiet, sir!"

So Blackie cuddled down in his chair, with one eye on his father and one eye on his mother, and both ears wide open. He could hardly eat a mouthful for listening about the house party. And he was *so* glad when Mrs. Blackrat said, "Well, my dear, I'll write the invitations this morning, and you may carry them to the city tonight. We will have the house party next week."

Mr. Blackrat looked over his glasses and said, "Suppose *you* take the invitations in to Madison Square, my dear. I think I could manage to keep house with Blackie while you are away."

You see, Mr. Blackrat was thinking about the big gray cat at Madison Square, only he did not like to say so. But Mrs. Blackrat said she did not feel well enough to go, and she did not like to leave Blackie. "Besides, I shall have the housecleaning to look after. I think you had better go, my dear."

"Very well, my dear, just as you wish," said Mr. Blackrat. And late that night he carried the invitations to the city. All of his friends at Madison Square were glad to see him, and crowded around him to hear about Mrs. Blackrat and little Blackie and the country home.

Then, when they had talked and talked, and it was time for Mr. Blackrat to think about starting home, they said, "Come into the pantry with us and have a little lunch before you go. The cook has just cut a new cheese today, and there is jelly and sponge cake and a pan of cream."

Mr. Blackrat's eyes sparkled. He hadn't tasted cheese since he moved to the country, and he was very fond of it. So he said, "I believe I will." Then down into the pantry all the rats skipped, as happy as they could be.

But just as Mr. Blackrat began to nibble a hole in the cheese, and the other rats were helping themselves to cream and jelly, the fat cook softly opened the pantry door, and blim! blim! blim! she whacked away with the kitchen broom. Away those rats scattered—pell-mell, helter-skelter, head over heels, one right after the other—Mr. Blackrat in the lead, always. You never saw such a sight in your life, and I tell you they were glad to get back to the garret.

"Goodness gracious me, my friends," said Mr. Blackrat, puffing and blowing, "what a life you must live! Why, I wouldn't live in the city for anything in the world! Maybe I don't get so many good things to eat in the country, but what I do get I can eat in peace, without getting my head whacked off by the cook, or bitten off by the cat. I'd rather go without cheese and jelly forever! My, how my heart thumps! I must go home. You all come out to the country and see us next week. You won't get your heads knocked off, I'm sure. Good-by; I must be going."

So off Mr. Blackrat went, as fast as he could trot, and when he got back to his quiet home in the country he felt very happy to know that he was safe once more. Mrs. Blackrat was glad to hear from her old friends again, and sure enough, the very next week they all came out to the house party. Everybody had a fine time, especially Blackie and

his little playmates, Ringtail, Snowwhite, and Brownie. They had the best
time of all. Blackie never got tired of

telling them about Mr. Lion. And Ringtail and Brownie and Snowwhite never got tired of listening. They didn't say one word about "imagination" either.

When the time came to go home, nobody wanted to go. "True," said little Snowwhite, "you don't have sponge cake and jelly to eat in the country—only peas and roots—but then, there is no big fat cook to knock your head off."

"And," said Blackie, "no big gray cat to—"

"Don't! Don't! Don't! Blackie! You know I cannot stand to hear you even call the name of that horrid gray cat! Don't! Don't!" said Mrs. Blackrat.

And Blackie hushed.

chapter six

The Gray Cat's Tricks

WHILE the rats were away at Mrs. Blackrat's house party, the big gray cat missed them very much. He couldn't tell *what* had become of them. The cook did not know, the rooster did not know, and even the little terrier dog could not tell. The big gray cat thought they must all be sick.

"Dear me, I hope it isn't mumps they have, or measles, or whooping cough," he said, as he stroked down the fur on his pretty white vest. "Mumps and

measles and whooping cough are catching. But what can be the matter with those rats? I haven't seen them for a week. Maybe the cook has been putting out rat poison. Surely she wouldn't do such a mean thing!"

And so the gray cat wondered and wondered.

Now the rats knew the gray cat was going to miss them while they were away at the house party. So they said, "Let's fool the gray cat, and not let him know when we get back from the country—maybe he will think we have gone away forever!"

Mr. Blackrat had given them a big bundle of peas and roots to carry home to the garret. When they got there, they were just as quiet as quiet could be. They did not go near the pantry for two or three whole days. They nibbled peas and roots, and roots and peas, hoping and hoping the gray cat would miss them so much he would go away to some other house to live.

But the old gray cat was very smart. He believed all along those rats were trying to fool him, and were hiding up in the garret. Sure enough, one day, while he was stretched out on the garden fence sunning, what should he see peeping at him from the attic window but the rats—every one of them!

"I thought so!" said the gray cat. "I thought so! Never mind, I know a trick or two myself. I will fool them. I'll play that I am dead, and they will come down to see—*then* I'll grab them sure!"

The gray cat tied a string to the fence, and hung to it by one hind leg. His eyes were shut tight and his head was hanging down. The rats were watching—

Snowwhite, Brownie, and Ringtail, every one. After a while little Snowwhite said, "Look, Brownie, I do believe the gray cat is dead. See how still he is, hanging there, and his eyes are shut *so* tight! I know he must be dead."

"I believe he is," said Brownie.

"I believe he is," said Ringtail.

"Oh, oh, oh! The gray cat is dead!" said all the rats. "Come, let's go down in the yard to play. We're not afraid now! The gray cat's dead! We know he is dead, because his eyes are shut!"

So every one of them ran laughing down the steps, right into the back yard. Ringtail even took a stick and poked the gray cat. Then, suddenly, *down* jumped the cat, with a great big dash. Fortunately for the rats he came down on the wrong side of the fence. If it had been the other side, one of those rats most surely would have been caught and gobbled up.

My, how they did scamper back up those garret steps—pell-mell, helter-skelter, head over heels, one right after the other!

The gray cat thought it was very funny. He laughed and said, "Never mind, I'll fool them again. Rats do not have very good memories—just wait until tomorrow."

And what do you think the gray cat did? The next day he jumped into a tub full of meal in the back yard, and covered himself with the meal. He left a little hole for his nose to breathe through— that was all.

He knew how much rats like to eat meal, and he kept just as still as still could be, so the rats would come down to the yard and jump into the tub. Then the gray cat thought he would surely catch them.

Ringtail was the first rat to see the meal, and he called all the other rats to the garret window, and they all came crowding and peeping over one another's shoulders to see the wonderful tub of meal.

Old Father Graybeard was the oldest

and the smartest rat of all. He said: "No, sir! I shall not jump into that tub! I've seen rattraps before today, and all of them are not made of wire, either! I believe that tub of meal is a rattrap and I believe the gray cat is hiding under the meal. But if Ringtail and Snowwhite and Brownie wish to go down to see, why, I'm willing!"

"You won't catch *me* going," said Brownie.

"You won't catch *me* going," said Ringtail.

"And you won't catch *me* going," said little Snowwhite.

"Very well," said Father Graybeard, "we will leave the meal for a while. If we see a hole in the meal the next time we look at it, we shall know that the gray cat was covered waiting for us to come." So, by and by, when Ringtail and Brownie and Snowwhite ran to the garret window to look again, there was a big hole right in the middle of that meal, and the gray cat was not anywhere to be seen.

"Oh-o!" said Snowwhite. "Just suppose we *had* gone down!"

"Oh-o!" said Ringtail.

"Oh-o!" said Brownie.

"I told you so!" said old Father Graybeard. "I told you so!"

chapter seven

Blackie and Mr. Bullfrog

MR. AND MRS. BLACKRAT were invited out to spend the day. Blackie was to stay at home and study his ABC's.

He wanted to go with his mother and father, but Mrs. Blackrat said, "No, Blackie. You always wiggle so! Be a good child now, and stay at home and study your A B C's. And remember, don't go anywhere—you hear?"

"Yes, Mother," said Blackie. Mrs. Blackrat did not allow Blackie to say, "Yes, ma'am," and "No, ma'am." She said it wasn't proper.

Well, after Mr. and Mrs. Blackrat went away, Blackie sat nodding over his A B C's. He always went to sleep when he studied them. He said he couldn't see any sense in them unless they spelled something like cat or rat. Anyway, just as he was nodding off, there came a big rap, tap, tap, at the front door. "Oh," said Blackie, "someone is knocking—someone has come to see me! Oh, how fine!"

So he ran down quickly to the door, and when he opened it there stood Mr. Bullfrog, all swelled out and dressed in a new green vest and spotted trousers.

Now, Mrs. Blackrat did not allow Blackie to play with frogs. She had

often told him they were rough and rude to rats, the way cats and dogs were, and they would surely bite if they got a chance. So he must never go with them. But there stood Mr. Bullfrog at Blackie's door, and he looked very polite and very smiling.

"Good morning, Blackie," said Mr. Bullfrog, with a low bow. "I knew you were by yourself this morning and might get lonely, so I've come to invite you down to my house, in the bottom of the pond. There are many beautiful things down there for you to see—pebbles and moss and shells. Wouldn't you like to go?"

"Oh, no," said Blackie, "I couldn't!

Mother told me not to. I do not know how to swim either. I would drown under the water."

"Pshaw!" said Mr. Bullfrog. "I'm a good frog. Your mother would be glad to have you go with me. Besides, I will hold you by the hand when we go through the water. You won't drown. What if you do get a little bit wet— your coat will soon dry off!"

"Oh, I can't," said Blackie. "Mother told me to study my A B C's."

"Nonsense!" said Mr. Bullfrog. "A B C's are no good! Come on. Your mother won't care, and I will give you some sponge cake and jelly."

Blackie liked sponge cake and jelly—

he thought it was the nicest thing in the world. He forgot all about what his mother had told him about Mr. Bullfrog, and how he might bite him if he got a chance. He just forgot everything but the sponge cake and jelly. He told Mr. Bullfrog he would go with him.

They started out, and pretty soon they stood on the bank of the pond, ready to jump in.

"Hold tight to my hind leg," said Mr. Bullfrog. "When I count three, jump! Ready! One, two, three!" Away went Blackie with a big splash into the water—down, down, down!

Oh, how it did scare him! The water got into his nose and eyes and mouth, and he wished and wished he had minded his mother and stayed at home.

"Let me go!" said Blackie. "I want to go back home!"

"No," said Mr. Bullfrog. "You can't go back home, ever. I've got you now, and I am going to keep you for my little rat."

"You won't," said Blackie. "I'm going back home to my mother. Let me go, I say!"

So Blackie pulled up and pulled up, while Mr. Bullfrog pulled down and pulled down. Mr. Bullfrog was so much stronger that he surely would have pulled Blackie down to the very bottom of the pond. But just then a big eagle flew over the pond and saw them.

Eagles like to eat frogs. So when Mr. Eagle saw Blackie and Mr. Bullfrog quarreling and pulling in the water, he swooped down and grabbed Mr. Bullfrog by the neck. Away he flew with Mr. Bullfrog, and with Blackie, too, for he was still hanging on to Mr. Bullfrog's hind leg.

Blackie was even more frightened now. It felt like he was going up to the moon! But just then Mr. Eagle gave such a big flap of his wings that Blackie let go of Mr. Bullfrog's hind leg. Down Blackie came, tumbling to the ground—over and over and over! Such a bump he got. He was so sore he could hardly hobble home, but he was glad to get there. Mrs. Blackrat had just come in and was putting away her Sunday bonnet. "Why, Blackie!" she said, "where have you been? You naughty, naughty child! Just look at your coat and face and hands! Where did you get so wet and muddy? I thought you were to stay at home and study your A B C's. What does this mean?"

Blackie felt very miserable. He wanted to cry, but he didn't.

He told his mother all about Mr. Bullfrog, and how he had promised him cake and jelly to go home with him, and then how the eagle had carried them both up in the air, and how he had been shaken off and came tumbling to the ground with a most dreadful bump. "Just see my bump, Mother," said Blackie. "Isn't it a big one?"

"A very good thing indeed, sir," said Mrs. Blackrat. "I like that bump! But you had better be glad that the eagle shook you off, or you might have been eaten up by now. The frog wished to do the very same thing to you that the eagle will do to him. It is a wonder that you ever got home alive—Blackie, Blackie, Blackie! I am ashamed that Mr. Bullfrog would tell a story about sponge cake and jelly. And I am ashamed that you would disobey your mother. Go wash your face and hands, sir, and go to bed without any supper."

chapter eight

Blackie at Madison Square

"MY DEAR," said Mr. Blackrat, "I must go into town on business to-night, to see about my life insurance papers. I think I shall take Blackie with me to make a little visit to Ringtail and Brownie and Snowwhite."

"Oh, don't go, Mr. Blackrat," said Mrs. Blackrat. "You know something will be sure to happen to Blackie if he goes. He is so wiggly and so restless the gray cat will be sure to get him. I shall not have one moment's peace while you are gone, for worrying over it. Please don't!"

But Blackie pleaded so hard, and promised to be so very careful, that at last his mother said he might go and stay three days.

Blackie was so happy he could hardly wait for the time to come. He had not been back to the big house on Madison Square since he had moved away, and he was very anxious to play in the garret once more.

When Mr. Blackrat started out Blackie ran with a hop and a skip by his side. When they reached the city and climbed the garret stairs, there were Ringtail and Brownie and Snowwhite.

Then what a fine time those little rats did have, playing and playing and playing. When bedtime came they were so tired that they cuddled up in the same little bed for a nap, and soon Ringtail and Brownie and Snowwhite were fast asleep.

But Blackie could not go to sleep. He was homesick. Suddenly, he heard music somewhere, soft and sweet and beautiful. Blackie wondered where it came from. He ran to the garret steps to listen. Then, before he knew what he was doing, he ran *down* the garret steps, following the sound of the music—on and on down a long, broad hall.

Then he came to a room with big folding doors, and right through the crack he crept. He had found the music, and his bright black eyes were full of joy. You didn't know rats liked music, did you? Well, they do, and Blackie was so carried away with it that he sat up on his hind legs in the corner and crossed his front legs, and wiggled his tail. He listened and listened and listened.

It was the little girl of the house who

was doing the playing. She sat at the piano practicing, counting softly, "One, two, three, four; one, two, three, four." Her feet just reached the pedals. She had soft brown curls and violet eyes and a sunny face.

By and by she looked over her shoulder to see what time it was. There in the corner she saw Blackie, sitting up on his hind legs, listening. She stopped playing to laugh, and Blackie scooted into the hall. But as soon as she began playing again, Blackie skipped back. He thought the music was so sweet he could listen to it always. The little girl played softly, on and on, watching Blackie over her shoulder.

All at once the hall door slammed. The noise frightened Blackie. He thought the gray cat had him. Away he ran, helter-skelter, pell-mell, up the garret steps, as he always did when he was frightened. How his heart did thump! But he cuddled down by little Snowwhite as still as still could be.

Then all was quiet, and he heard no more music. The little girl had finished her practice, and had gone to tell her mother about the queer little rat who sat in the corner to hear her play.

chapter nine

Blackie in the Trap

BLACKIE had one more day to stay at Madison Square, then Mr. Blackrat was coming to take him home. Blackie and Brownie and Ringtail and Snow-white wanted to have all the fun they could. They had been sitting up in the sunny window seat, listening to Father Graybeard talk about traps.

He told them about every kind of rat-trap he could think of, so they would be careful and never get caught in one.

"Yes, sir," said Father Graybeard,

"you little rats had better be careful. Listen to your elders, or *you'll* get caught in a trap some day."

They said they would be careful. Then they ran off up the side of the wall to play "hiding." By and by Brownie said, "I'm just as hungry as hungry can be; let's go down to the pantry to find something nice to eat."

And Ringtail and Snowwhite and Blackie said, "Yes, let's go."

So off they scampered to the pantry. There were pies and cream and jelly cake on the pantry shelf. Down on the floor Blackie saw a queer little wire house, with an open wire chimney to it. Inside the little house there was a big piece of fresh cheese.

"We'd better not touch it," said Snowwhite. "That wire house *might* be one of those traps Father Graybeard told us about."

"Pshaw," said Blackie, "I don't believe it! That is just a piece of cheese the cook doesn't want. I'm going in to eat it. The door is open, and so is the chimney."

Before Snowwhite could say another word, Blackie went down the chimney of the little wire house. Sure enough, it was a trap, and when Blackie got in he couldn't get out.

"Oh-o!" said Ringtail, "Blackie's gone now!"

"Oh-o!" said Snowwhite, "I told you so, Blackie!"

Then Brownie said, "Hush, I hear somebody coming." The cook opened the pantry door, and away ran Brownie and Snowwhite and Ringtail—one right after the other—up the garret steps. Blackie was all by himself and in the trap.

"Ah, yes," said the fat cook, as she stooped down to look in the trap, "I've got you now! You are the very rat that has been eating up my pies and cakes.

Who invited you into my pantry, I'd like to know?"

Blackie was too scared to say a word. He just sat up on his hind legs and crossed his front paws, as his mother told him to when he wanted to say "Please." The fat cook laughed. Then she stepped to the pantry door and called, "Dorothy! Oh, Dorothy! Run here quickly! I've something to show you."

Blackie heard a door open, and a pair of feet came dancing down the hall. In rushed a little girl, the same little girl that Blackie had seen playing the piano.

"Oh my," she said, stooping down by the side of the wire cage. "What are you going to do with this dear little rat?"

"Why, I'm going to give him to the gray cat," said the fat cook.

"Oh, please don't!" said Dorothy. "This is the same little rat that watched me practice the other night. See how he holds his front paws, and how cute he is sitting on his hind legs. Oh, give him to me, please!"

At first the cook shook her head and said, "No." Then she said, "Yes," and handed the trap to Dorothy.

Dorothy looked at Blackie for a while, and then she opened the trap door. Blackie raced out and up the garret steps, happier than he had ever been before.

Blackie never again went near another rattrap. For, as Father Graybeard had told them, "Little rats have to be caught before they learn what rattraps are. They will not believe their elders."

Pretty soon Mr. Blackrat came and took Blackie home to the country. When Blackie curled up by his mother's side, he told her all about the pretty music he had heard, and the wire trap, and the little girl who had saved his life.

And what do you suppose his mother said? Why, she wouldn't believe him! She just said, "Blackie, hush! Your imagination is something terrible!"

chapter ten

Blackie's Picnic

IT WAS one night while his mother was putting him to bed that Blackie begged to go out in the woods and have a picnic all by himself.

"Why, Blackie," said Mrs. Blackrat, "How strange you are. Who ever heard of having a picnic all by yourself?"

"Please, Mother, do," said Blackie, patting her on the cheek, "just this once! I'll be *so* good!"

So Mrs. Blackrat said, "Well, go right to sleep and hush talking, and I will see about it in the morning."

"What does 'see about it' mean, Mother? Does it mean 'yes'?" said Blackie.

"I guess so, if it doesn't rain," said Mrs. Blackrat. "Now, not another word; go right to sleep."

So Blackie shut his eyes, and the next time he opened them it was daylight. It wasn't raining, and sure enough, Mrs. Blackrat gave Blackie a lunch and he started off on the picnic. As he skipped

away she kept squealing out to him,
"Now, be careful! Don't fall! Don't
go near the water! Don't tear your coat!
Don't stay out late! Don't—"

But Blackie did not hear the last
"don't," because he was too far away.
"I wish Snowwhite and Ringtail and
Brownie could come on my picnic, too,"
Blackie said to himself.

He had a very good
time. He played all the
morning with leaves
and flowers and grass,
and when dinnertime
came he spread his
lunch on a rock by a
spring. There were

roasted peas, a baked potato root, and a slice of dried apple.

"Such a good mother," said Blackie, "to give me this tasty lunch!" After dinner he played again. Then he ran down a little path to hunt wild strawberries to carry home for Mr. and Mrs. Blackrat's supper.

"Poor Mother and Father!" said Blackie, "they couldn't come to my picnic. I will take them something good." While he was hunting berries he came to a very queer house with a tiny crack in it, just large enough for Blackie to squeeze through.

"Oh-o," said Blackie. "A house full of corn! I believe I won't hunt for any more strawberries. I will stay here and eat some of this corn. Then I will carry some home. Won't Mother be glad!" When he tasted the corn, it was so good he ate and ate until he couldn't eat any more! Then he just curled up in a nest of corn and went sound asleep. When Blackie woke up, he had slept such a long time the moon was shining. It was nighttime!

"Oh-o, what will Mother do with me!" said Blackie. "She told me not to stay out late. I must hurry home as fast as I can. She might think I am lost."

He hurried to the tiny crack, but though he squeezed and squeezed, he couldn't get through. "What makes me so *fat?*" said Blackie. "This is the door I came through this afternoon. Why can't I get out now?"

Well, Mrs. Blackrat waited and waited for Blackie. When he didn't come home to supper she did not know what to think. "Blackie shall never go on another picnic," said Mrs. Blackrat. "I told him not to stay out late. The moon is shining, and he has still not come home! We must look for him, Mr. Blackrat. You go one way and I will go the other."

So they looked and looked for Blackie, and then Mrs. Blackrat began to cry. She said she knew Blackie had tumbled into the water and been drowned, and she never would see him any more.

But Mr. Blackrat said, "Oh, no, my dear. Don't cry and say such things as that. Blackie is just lost; he is a bright little fellow and will find his way home. You go to bed and I will look for Blackie."

Mrs. Blackrat said she couldn't go to sleep with Blackie lost in the woods in the dark night. She trotted on by the side of Mr. Blackrat, looking everywhere for Blackie.

By and by they came to the spring, and saw the rock where Blackie had eaten his dinner. They knew that because crumbs of roasted peas, potato root and dried apple were there.

Next they found the little path twisting through the woods, and some tiny footprints in the sand. Mr. Blackrat said, "Whose tracks are these, I wonder?"

"Why, they are Blackie's tracks!" said Mrs. Blackrat, hopping up and down with joy. "I'd know Blackie's tracks anywhere—they are the most beautiful tracks in the world! Hurry, hurry, Mr. Blackrat. You are so slow!"

She ran on ahead of Mr. Blackrat, just as fast as she could go, following the little tracks in the sand. Sure enough, they led right up to the little crack in the corn-house. And there stood Blackie, with only his head peeping through.

Mrs. Blackrat was so happy she did not know what to do, so she sat on a stone and fanned herself. Mr. Blackrat couldn't do a thing but laugh when he saw Blackie was so fat he couldn't get through the crack.

"You little rascal," he said. "Now aren't you a pretty sight! Why don't you come out of that door and meet your mother?"

"I c-a-n't!" said Blackie. "I don't know why. I came in all right, but when I started home—"

"You were so very fat you couldn't squeeze through," said Mr. Blackrat. "I wonder how much of that corn you have eaten."

"Why, Blackie," said Mrs. Blackrat, "I am ashamed of you! To think that a son of mine could be so greedy! Blackie, don't you touch another grain of that corn. Not another grain, sir, until you have lost enough of that fat to squeeze

85

through the crack, you wretched child! Blackie, throw me out a few grains of that corn, and let me see how it tastes!"

It took a long time for Blackie to lose weight, and he got very hungry. But Mrs. Blackrat would not let him taste a thing—not even a grain of corn. Finally he lost enough weight so that he was thin enough to squeeze through the little crack. Then he was the happiest little rat in the world. And Blackie never went through any more little cracks, unless he was very sure he could get out again.

chapter eleven

Blackie's Egg

ON SUNDAY afternoons Blackie
and Mr. Blackrat always went out
walking. Mrs. Blackrat liked to take a
Sunday nap. She couldn't sleep very well
when Blackie was there, because she said
he wiggled and talked so much. But Mr.
Blackrat said that was just because
Blackie did not have anything else to do,
so they just went out walking.

Blackie was always finding something
pretty as he hopped on ahead of Mr.
Blackrat. By and by he came to a hollow

stump in the fence corner and found a fine fresh egg—but Blackie thought it was a rock!

"Why-y," said Mr. Blackrat, "that's no rock. That's a hen's egg, and it is very good to eat."

Mr. Blackrat's eyes twinkled and twinkled.

But just at that very minute he heard something growling and running through the woods. "What can it be, Father?" said Blackie. "It does not sound like Mr. Lion."

"No, indeed," said Mr. Blackrat. "Let me see!"

He scrambled up on the fence to look. Then he scrambled down again very

Clara Atwood Fitts

quickly, saying, "Run, run, my son, it's Mr. Fox. He is coming this way, and looks very angry. Hurry! Run, run!"

"Oh, Father," said Blackie, "run and leave our egg! Can't we carry it home? Then Mother can help us eat it."

Mr. Blackrat did not want to leave the nice egg either. He tried to get it up on his back, but he couldn't. Then he tried to hold it in his front legs, and he tried to hold it in his hind legs, but every time it would slip. "Well," said Mr. Blackrat, "we will just have to leave it. Too bad, too bad!"

Then Blackie thought of a plan. "Quick, Father, quick!" he said. "I know what we can do. I can be a little wagon—my tail can be the handle. You drag me, while I lie on my back and hold the egg."

"To be sure," said Mr. Blackrat. "Why, you've got more sense than I thought you had. But won't it hurt?"

"Oh, I guess it will scratch me up a little," said Blackie, "But that doesn't matter. Pull away—here we go!"

So Mr. Blackrat caught Blackie's tail, while he lay on his back and held tight to the egg. And away they went, bumpty, bumpty, bump, across the grass. Mr. Fox was right after them. But he couldn't catch Mr. Blackrat; he ran too fast for that, and the egg didn't get broken either.

"Mercy!" said Mrs. Blackrat when she saw them coming. "Mercy on me! What *do* you mean, Mr. Blackrat, coming home in this disgraceful fashion? On Sunday, too! Why, have you both gone crazy?"

Then she saw the egg, and how she did smile! She wasn't angry any more, and said she didn't care if Blackie did soil his Sunday coat. It could be washed again.

They certainly did have a good Sunday supper that night. It was the nicest supper they had eaten in a long, long time.